Three-Alarm FIRE!

By Annie Auerbach   Illustrated by Joe Ewers & Steve Mitchell

LITTLE SIMON
An imprint of Simon & Schuster Children's Publishing Division
New York   London   Toronto   Sydney   Singapore
1230 Avenue of the Americas
New York, New York 10020

Manufactured in the United States of America
First Edition
2 4 6 8 10 9 7 5 3 1
ISBN 0-689-85897-3

David Donshel arrived at the Hero City fire station at exactly eight A.M. After going through extensive training this was his first day as a firefighter.

"David!" someone called. It was Fred Klein, the fire captain. "Good to have you as part of the team."

"Thank you, sir," David replied. "It's great to be here."

"Come on, I'll introduce you to everyone," said Fred.

ENGINE Co. 71

David met the other firefighters. The Hero City station had two teams: the engine company, whose truck had water pumps and hoses to put out fires, and the ladder company, which was responsible for search and rescue. David was going to be part of the ladder company.

A firefighter named Melissa showed David around the station, including where they ate and slept.

"Welcome to your home away from home," Melissa joked, since firefighters work twenty-four-hour shifts at a time.

David looked around as Adam was inspecting the fire engine. He told David about all of the hoses and pumps on the vehicle. Even though David's specialty was search and rescue, he was still curious about fire engines.

"Hey, don't go trading companies," James teased David. James was a firefight for the ladder company. He was responsible for maintaining the fire truck.

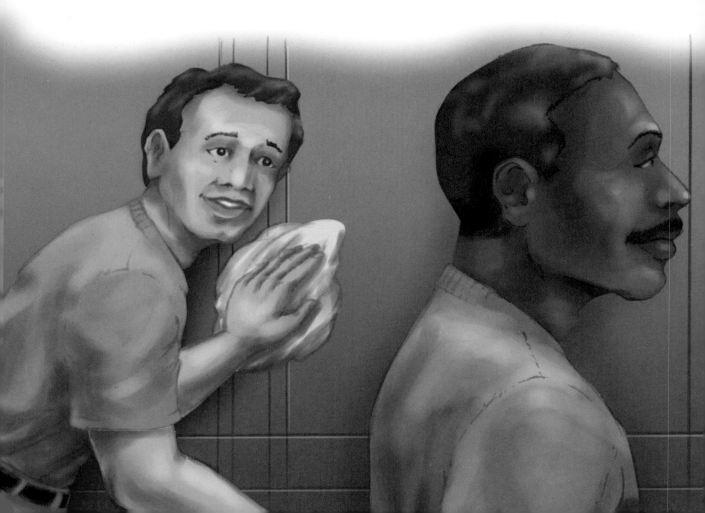

The firefighters had a friendly rivalry. They loved to tease each other.

"Oh, come on," said Adam. "Your ladders are no match for my engine. I hav[e] tank that can hold up to one thousand gallons of water!"

"We have more than just ladders," James said proudly. "We have a toolbox o[n] wheels."

Then David jumped into the conversation. "Just remember, Adam: Firefighters on't only put out fires. They also do search and rescue."

James laughed. "That's right! How is that tank of water going to help you then?"

"I know how you can use some water," Fred said. He walked over to the group rrying a bucket and sponge and asked David to wash the ladder truck. "Think of as your initiation to being part of the team!"

Suddenly the alarm bell rang. The firefighters jumped into action. They hurried to put on their protective gear. Then Fred grabbed the incident report sent by the dispatcher. There was a huge traffic accident on the highway, and a woman was trapped in her car!

It was a job for the ladder company, the experts at search and rescue!

Less than a minute after the alarm bell rang the fire truck pulled out of the station with the siren wailing. Drivers pulled over or stood still as the fire truck went around their cars.

Sitting in the jump seat, David was nervous and excited. It was his first official call!

The fire truck arrived on the scene. A car and a truck had crashed into each other, sending them into the center divider on the freeway. Worst of all, a woman was trapped in her car! The firefighters immediately began their rescue mission.

"Let's try the crowbar," said James.

But it wasn't working. They would have to use a special heavy-duty tool. David moved at lightning speed. Before long he and James had pried open the of of the car. The woman trapped inside was eased out. Then Melissa, who was a medic, examined the woman for any possible injuries.

"Nice job, David," James said afterward. "You worked really quickly."

"Thanks," David replied. "I remember the very first thing I learned in training: 'Every second counts in an emergency!'"

"The number one rule in fire fighting!" agreed James.

That evening David and the other firefighters made dinner at the station since their shift didn't end until the next morning.

"So what do you think of your first day?" James asked David.

"Not bad," replied David. "Although I can't wait to confront my first fire."

"Oh, don't worry," said James. "You'll have plenty of chances!"

James was right. At five-fifteen A.M. the firefighters were woken up by the alarm sounding. Since they slept in their clothes, it only took them a minute to slide down the pole, put on their protective gear, and jump on to their trucks.

Both the engine company and the ladder company were called for this emergency. It was a three-alarm fire!

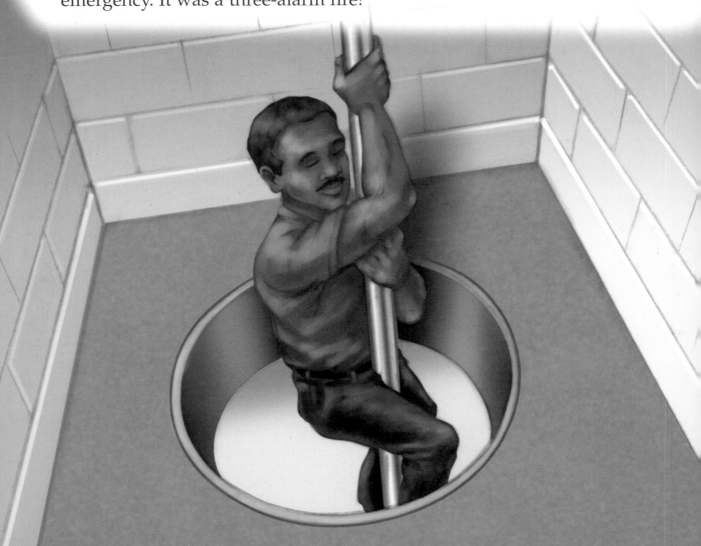

The sirens blared, and the fire truck and fire engine raced through the streets.

On board each vehicle the firefighters prepared themselves to face the blaze. They put on the tanks and masks that would give them each thirty minutes of air.

At the scene the firefighters saw flames engulfing a four-story house. Without a moment to lose, the firefighters did their tasks. Fred, the fire captain, was in charge of coordinating everyone to put out the fire as quickly and safely as possible. David and the rest of the ladder company raised a ladder up to the roof. Once they were up there, they carefully cut holes in the roof with axes, so trapped smoke could get out.

Meanwhile the engine company unloaded hoses and hooked them up to fire hydrants.

Whoosh!

The water came blasting out of the hoses. There was so much power and pressure that it took two firefighters to hold each hose!

"David, lead the search and rescue team!" Fred ordered and David sprang into action. It was his team's job to make sure no one was still inside the house.

As each firefighter searched a room he put an **X** with chalk on the bottom of the door. This would save essential time.

In the last room David found an elderly man. He swiftly led the man to safety outside the house.

"Melissa!" called David. "I think he's suffering from smoke inhalation."

"I'm on it," she responded and took the man to the waiting ambulance.

But David's job was not over yet! Fred ordered the ladder company to start using the hoses at the top of the building.

"Let's use the aerial ladder," said James. "David, do you want to go up?"

"Sure!" replied David as he climbed into the bucket attached to the end of the ladder.

Eventually the fire was put out—much to the relief of the neighbors.

"Good work, everyone," Fred told the firefighters. And to David, he said, "Welcome to the family."

The tired firefighters made their way back to the station.